Curious George®

Piñata Party

Adaptation by Marcy Goldberg Sacks and Priya Giri Desai
Based on the TV series teleplay written by Craig Miller

Houghton Mifflin Harcourt
Boston 2009

Library of Congress Cataloging-in-Publication Data is on file.
ISBN-13: 978-0-547-11962-5

Design by Afsoon Razavi and Marcy Goldberg Sacks

www.houghtonmifflinbooks.com

Printed in China
WKT 10 9 8 7 6 5 4 3 2 1

George was having fun.
It was Betsy's birthday party.
There were many new things to see
and do.

George heard a wind chime.
He looked up.
A paper animal hung from a tree.
Up close, it smelled sweet.

“That’s a piñata,” said Betsy.
“There is candy inside.”
George had to hit the piñata to get
the candy out.

George wore a blindfold.
He could not see.
He swung, but he kept missing the piñata.

Steve had an idea.
"Practice using your other senses," he said.
"Try to follow Charkie with the blindfold on."

George could not see.
But he could hear.
George followed the barking.

But the city was noisy.
George could not always hear Charkie.
So he used his hands to feel what was
around him.

Click-click.
Charkie's collar made noise.
George followed the sound.
Charkie hid in the fire station.
George felt cold metal.
It was a truck.
He turned on the hose by mistake!
Everything got very wet.

The firefighters turned off the hose.
Now George could smell a wet dog.
He kept chasing Charkie.

Now George felt fur.
Meow! It was his friend Gnocchi.

Mmm . . . George smelled yummy food.
Then he heard Charkie's collar again.

Click-click! George chased Charkie through the kitchen.

He followed the noisy collar.
Soon there was less city noise.
They were in Endless Park.
George felt wet fur.
He found his doggy friend!

They went back to the party.
George wanted to swing at the
piñata again.

George could not see, so he used his other senses.
He heard the wind chime in the tree.
He felt the grass under his toes.

He also smelled candy.
George moved to the piñata.
BAM!
Candy flew everywhere.
Now George could use his sense of TASTE.
That was the best one to use at a birthday party!

Explore Your World

In the story, George uses his senses to find the piñata. Use your senses in the fun experiments below. You will need an adult to help you put on a blindfold first. Now, no peeking!

SMELL

1. Have an adult place five different foods in separate bowls in front of you. These should be foods that have strong smells, such as garlic, cheese, pickles, and oranges.
2. Lift each bowl up, without touching what is inside, and take a good long sniff.
3. Can you guess which food it is by its odor?

Record how many you guessed correctly here: ☐

TASTE

1. Have an adult cut up five different foods and place them in separate bowls. These should be foods that have tastes you know, such as grapes, apples, carrots, and cucumbers.
2. Using a fork so you aren't touching the food with your hands, can you guess which foods they are just by tasting them?
3. **Challenge:** Do the same thing with foods you have tasted only once or twice before!

Record how many you guessed correctly here: ☐

TOUCH

1. Have an adult place five different foods in separate bowls. These should be foods that you can feel and recognize, such as spaghetti, ice cream, uncooked rice, and hard-boiled eggs.
2. Can you guess which foods they are just by touching them?

   Record how many you guessed correctly here: ☐

The next time you go to your favorite park, take a look around you. Where are the trees? Where are the flowers? Make a list of everything you see. Now wear a blindfold, and with the help of a grownup, try to find those things. Use your senses of smell, touch, and hearing to remember where all those objects are. When you're done, take off the blindfold and see how well you did.

Your Senses and You

Fill in the blank with the correct part of your body. Just like George, you use your senses every day!

1. I use my ____________ to look at pictures.

2. I use my ____________ to smell flowers.

3. I use my ____________ to feel a cat's fur.

4. I use my ____________ to hear a bell ring.

5. I use my ____________ to taste an ice cream cone.

Which sense would you use?

You're in your room playing, and you feel hungry. Your dad is making dinner in the kitchen. How do you know what he is cooking?

You're at the park and you are playing with your friend. How do you know when it's time to go home?

Answers: (1) eyes (2) nose (3) hands (4) ears (5) tongue
(A) By smelling the food. (B) By hearing your mom say, "Let's go!"